AF581593

BARELY LEGAL

THE COLLECTED
DREAM BOY BOOK CLUB
Vol. 2

ISBN: 979-8-9920663-4-0
Catalog Number: DBBC016

Editor: Jonathan Blake Fostar
All work previously appeared in DBBC Series 5-8.

dreamboybook.club
USA

TABLE OF CONTENTS

Intro to *BARELY LEGAL*

Jonathan Blake Fostar

Pussy and poetry have rotted my brains.

Whatever. It's holy. Sort of. There are worse ways to go. There's pancreatic cancer. There's being burned at the stake. I used to be so much smarter before grad school.

Now my head is just smushed up Blink-182 lyrics and pictures of belly-button rings.

Don't be scared, my dude. All the poets of the future will be laptops anyways. It's okay. We can still fuck shit up. I fucked up yesterday. I don't want to talk about it. People still like me.

It's easy to be hot when you're 18. It's easy to write a poem when there's nothing at stake. It's easy to be brave when everything is just plot or you are made of plastic. Talk to me in ten years. Talk to me when your teeth fall out. Talk to me when the sag sets in.

Everybody knows an algorithm will write the next great American novel. 10/10. Five stars.

Do something else instead. Something stupid. We have to be more illegal. Equations can't make mistakes quite like we can.

You have tools, girl, you have weapons. Your cellphone is a machine gun. Hotness is so human. War is coming. No fluff. Are you down? Cause I'm down. I'm kinda always down.

The technology will break. Books will be burned. Everybody will forget everything eventually.

Literature is temporary. Being hot is forever.

So thank god baddies keep typing away. Fingering their navels. Lighting small fires. Can't you see the tramp stamps? They glow in the dark. Aren't they pretty? Amen, bro. Amen!

Here come the angels.

Pony Girl

Madlen Stafford

I dreamed last night that millions of shooting stars began falling to Earth right before us. Our eyes so wide, and hands so cold. There was so much swirling and burning. When the stars exploded Pony Girl's face gleamed so orange, and even brighter than her strawberry hair. Embers of stardom twinkled upon us. One hundred little explosions chased us down Rabbit Hill, through my driveway, up the stairs, and behind the door of my childhood bedroom. The door with the peeling blue paint, faint inscriptions, and a hole punched through it. The explosions tucked us into bed at night.

Traveling to Earth ignites a flame,
nurses it. I will thrill myself on the joys of flailing.

***

I will text back. I will go. I will stay. I will walk alone through a snowy day...my hands through my blouse and on my chest. I will be a contortionist. My dress is black, and taller than I. I will stay. I will think about "Naked" by Mike Leigh all day without watching it. I will remember that I like to have sex like that. I will bend. I will defend stupid opinions, impress you. I will not be like her. I will pity myself, lay on the floor. I will imagine God was not watching us when

I scratched the years off of her ID and replaced them with mine. I will twirl on thin ice. I will be an ugly apartment, broken floor. I will flood. I will be whatever names I am called today. I will go where I am sought; Be that near or far. I will let the glow of your mother's kitchen cabinet lights in rural suburbia guide me through your night...not mine. I will dream of jumping on mattresses, her tattered rouge tights. I will overfill myself with tears. I will be navy blue, fading black.

***

Loon birds varying in size invite their evening by tracing wake trails through the pond akin to those of my father's Jon boat. I miss my friend. I miss her so much. Pony Girl. Her hair grew longer than mine in the year when my days stopped. She wears red lipstick to sleep every night and sometimes eyeliner on special occasions. Her favorite song was always "I Love How You Love Me." My mother always told me if I do one thing it's to tell the truth. Pony Girl tells me that she wants to be alive again, and I tell her that she is.

Our days are: Hardened feet, cold blue eyes, waiting in life for the restroom, waiting on the platform for a train, waiting alone at an empty station, nursing the bottle in bed...rooftops...a little sister's treehouse, a scrunched ankle sock below the bed, dad's old truck, grandma's pup, the lake when we were floating-staring at the sky, a dismal southern room illuminated by the light of a violent video game, one ear to a closed door and the other one covered, yellow bathing suits, Pony Girl's toothy smile, seven years old too many chocolate ice cream bars.

strawberry mango

Sahaj Kaur

i fell in love with a guy because he ubered me
home from the old bar

i can't visualize his face

even though i had my own side to his bed

i shouldn't be left around applebee's margarita
buckets

i'll drunk text before 9 pm

i used to be psychic but all i could predict

about you was when you would tell me to get
down on my knees

i liked you

even though you called american spirit blues
greens

and the fact you have red scare premium
either makes you a pervert or a girl

the first night i met you i whispered in your ear

"i'd do whatever u told me to"

and you plopped an olive in my mouth

god is a 34 year old man and he smokes
strawberry mango elfbars

Doomsday

Eva Catherine Kuhn

About a minute after the end of the world, Mouse started to fidget. She wondered if the clock was behind. Wolf told the girl to shut her damn mouth. The five sat cross-legged on the floor of a tapestry-draped room, heavy with the odors of marijuana and sweat. Four believers were clad in white, while Wolf, the skinny, thirty-something-year-old-Prophet, was dressed in glimmering silver chainmail. It was December 21st: the clock had just struck midnight. Instead of hellfire and the agonized screams of the unenlightened, the strange group was met with only the sound of the old heater kicking to life.

At 12:04, Bear was the first to move. Wordlessly, the man left the pentacle, took his bag from the couch, and walked out the door. Frog's neck snapped between his increasingly red-faced leader and the spot where Bear had once sat. Kittie, with her slow-blinking eyes, gazed uncommittedly at the ceiling. Mouse was on the verge of tears, her bottom lip quivering. She sniffled. No one spoke. They heard from outside the newspaper-covered window as Bear's truck started up and tore down the driveway. The others would never see him again.

At 12:07, Wolf shot up so suddenly that even Kittie jumped. He threw himself against a bookshelf. He clawed at his throat, his face twisting and contorting. Then, he crashed to the floor, convulsing. Mouse shrieked, kneeling before him and trying in vain to grab his arms. Frog stood, but his legs wouldn't walk. He noticed Kittie wasn't moving.

"Don't just stand there!" Mouse begged Frog. "Help me hold him down!"

Frog looked to Kittie for what to do. Her face, sharp and genuinely cat-like with curled sweeps of dark eyeliner, betrayed nothing. Before Wolf, Kittie was Elena, a student at the University. Frog sometimes passed her on campus when he was leaving the lab. Those memories, though only a few months old, felt like they belonged to another lifetime.

"A message," Wolf spat out between the gibberish. He began to slam his head back against the floor. Hysterical, Mouse tore from the room. She returned with a pillow and shoved it beneath her dear leader's head. Wolf just rolled over and went right on doing the same thing. Frog felt as if he might throw up. He wished the world had ended like it was supposed to. At least then he wouldn't have to deal with this.

Outside, the night was clear, and a big silver moon reflected from a blanket of glittering, white snow. In seven or so hours, the sun would rise. The world would wake up. He could still go home, Frog found himself thinking, and make it back to Iowa in time for Christmas Eve. He could see his little sister.

"Don't be an idiot, Frog," Kittie hissed. It was 12:10 A.M. "Hold him down so we can hear what God has to say."

Carrie

Stella Parker

feeling cute and peaceful
like carrie before the blood
i go all out
trying on compassion
at the party with my enemy
doing no harm
then finding jesus
on a tuesday
he told me it's ok
bitch

Daddy Miami

Madison Murray

In Miami, it's beautiful like Xanadu. Men drive cockily, everyone's a sugar baby, and children don't exist. David, my sugar daddy, says he likes "docile women" but somehow still likes me most. Every chance I get, I remind him that "my dad just died." I'm wicked paranoid: of being outed, of being trafficked, of my father's ghost haunting me. I call my therapist from a beach chair and she tells me to take niacin for paranoia and to imagine my dad's soul on an island. As a prisoner there, he must relive his life through his daughters' eyes. If he ever learns anything, he will be able to move onto the next life. It still won't be a great life. Maybe he'll be a worm or the last shit I ever take.

My First Khole

Carmen Llin

We were in a basement. There were groupies and there were DJs. The groupies were silly. The DJs even more so. I was the silliest of them all. I didn't know how to hold the straw. The groupies were glaring at me.

They don't think I'm silly. They think I'm *RETARDED*. And I feel ashamed.

Silly is an acronym.

Silly stands for "Silly I love LOVE you".

Retarded only means *ily* when I call u a *retard*.

Retarded is a word u can't say outside of Dimes Square without getting cancelled.

Smoking was not allowed. And we all smoked. We all smoked A LOT. And the blunts didn't work btw.

I am immune to drugs. The first time I did K I was happy but I didn't khole.

I am a kitten. We do cocaine. It does not work. It makes me sleepy. It makes me want to read u 1000 poems. I read u the raped nun's confession from *Bad Lieutenant*. U film me. *Wait this is not the good part. Wait. What. I lost the plot.*

We go to ur Airbnb. For a couple of days I forget I might be pregnant. I ask u to fuck me *rlly* hard so that I'll stop being pregnant. *Baby we lost the baby.* It was not yours :'c

I love you and I love doing drugs with u. I won't get addicted to drugs tho. I am addicted to nothing and drugs are too much. And I don't wanna get pimples and stuff.

We do more cocaine and put little balls of dust into two cigarettes. There is enough dust on ur phone to do one more line each. But you throw away the rest of the cocaine. You blow it away like a candle. You say it's important for you. You have to blow it away so that cocaine does not become important. I go doe eye coquette fawn waif mode in hopes u won't blow it away. U say I'm a junkie. I say I have post war mentality. I lick your fingers. I wanna lick ur phone. You cannot throw away things like that.

My grandmother had a cabinet filled with free sugar bags. Then she died. And she hated me. And she had a cabinet filled with free sugar bags. I still cry about the civil war and other wars I'm too stupid or privileged to know about. I cry about babies dying. I cry about being ugly. I cry about being fat. I cry about being stupid. I cry about being bad and i want my imaginary baby to die. Not only do i want it to die, i want it not to exist. I'm sorry mom. I have a baby and it lives in a Schrodinger box. I don't care whether it exists or not. I don't want it to exist. I hate myself for having a little Schrodinger's cat inscribed onto my belly.

We go outside to smoke the cigarettes lined with coke. It's 3am and there's weird people on the street. I'm not scared bc I'm the girl and girls must be protected and always have been protected. But you have seen some fucked up shit in your life so the weird people on the street are not funny to you.

Then we go back to the room. We do half a gram of K each. You teach me how to use a straw. My fur coat smells like drugs bc your nose smells like drugs. There is white dust on your hair and on your shirt. There is dust on my white tennis skirt but u can't see it bc it's white. I'm stupid and I'm white and I should not say the nword.

We put two chairs facing each other. Then I sit on your lap. We look into each other's eyes -uwu- Your eyes are lighter than I thought. You look like a cat. But not a normal one. One of those Dasha likes. The ones that live in the snow. (rip dash snow)

We run to the bed to charge our phones before the K hits. I think it won't ever hit. I've never kholed. My brain is broken. You put an episode of *Rick and Morty* on your phone. But the ketamine hits and this is corny but I get lost in your body. It stops being a body and becomes an infinite spiral building. Your shirt is dark and the lights are off. The rooms in your body are dark but I know they are not empty. There are calico critters running inside of u. I am a calico critter but I move very slowly. I bump into them. They are running. They are afraid.

When we die we'll all go to the same place. When we die we'll all go to heaven. Heaven is heaven for good people and heaven is scary for people like me. I wonder as I walk through the dark corridors of heaven if I am in heaven. There must be more than one heaven. No, heaven must be the ultimate singularity. What if heaven feels like a stupid instagram reel. Can I accept heaven. Am I pure enough to accept heaven. Can I live here forever. Could I find God in heaven. Would I dare to say *haiiii >w<.*

I become tiny and tinier like a molecule. I keep getting lost. I look for your heart because I know it's not empty. I become so small I think I can find God. I look for God inside your body forever. Forever stops. I exit the spiral building. I realize it's your body.

I lose my mother tongue. I realize we are in a room. I realize ur here. Ur head is wonky. Ur an adorable giant. I am a microbe but still realize I have a body. I am an atom but my eyes are bigger than my flesh. My eyes become so big they stop working. And I think having a body is weird. Being alive is so weird. BEING ALIVE IS SO WEIRD. I still can't believe this is the same body I had as a child. I'm not a child. I'm still that child. This is the same flesh I had as a child. How can I feel so alien from that child. Would she hate me. AM I PRETTY. I am about to die and this is all that matters. 'IM SO FUCKING UGLY. THIS IS SO FUCKING UGLY. Ur with me. I lose my tongue. I'm afraid to make you sad. So I write whatever this is so u can't hear it.

"This is so fucking disgusting no actually its beautiful everything is so fucking ugly every thing is so fucking beautiful being alive fw-wls soo weird idk who i am Gravity and Grace grace."

I don't want you to think ur ugly bc ur beautiful and you are good. Everything is ugly because I am ugly. I am disgusting and therefore should not contaminate true beauty. everything is so beautiful rn that the rest feels so ugly I have to say it out loud.

My fingers don't work. I crawl out of bed. I get on my knees. What if I die rn. My mom would not know where I am. It would be an inconvenience for you and you would be cancelled. I'm ready to die but I won't bc u care and so does my mom. This is not the place where I'll die.

I won't let my body die. I can't die in an Airbnb. I can't die on kitty valium and I can't die in this city bc how cringe.

So I bow my head between ur legs and talk to my mommy in heaven. Virgin Mary forgive me FORGIVE ME FORGIVE ME FORGIVE ME. Forgive me for doing drugs forgive me for lying to my mom forgive me for wanting to die forgive me for having sex forgive me for smoking cigarettes forgive me for raping myself forgive me for being bad even though I know how to be good. Forgive me bc saying sorry is not enough. Forgive me bc I know I won't change. Forgive me for changing so much. Forgive me for killing myself as a child. Saying sorry is not enough.

I feel so close to God rn bc I'm so high. Drugs are sinful but I feel so close to u rn. I don't want to forget.

I see your face and the room starts getting small again. We've retarded ourselves back to creation. I can feel creation and it feels like death. We could have sex at the end of creation but we still don't have a body so u don't have a dick and I don't have a pussy and I don't have a dick and u don't have a pussy and I'm all bleeding eyes and your skin is too soft to touch without breaking it and like god we don't have a body but we are not god so if we tried to have sex without a body we would die.

I come back to material heaven. Everything is big but I can see now. Ur still tripping. You say ur having a bad trip. I ask why. You say ur afraid. Of what. Ur afraid of pain. I'm scared of pain too but I must be ur guardian angel now. So I say: *pain is a sensation and all sensations must be enjoyed.* I read that on tumblr when I was 14. But I'm scared of pain too. Pain is not the same as self-harm or bdsm. It comes as a shock when you don't want it and it does not leave u a pretty scar.

If you choked me to death, I would not feel pain. Pain rapes u again and again and you become uglier each time with each rape and each rape is the first and you will be a virgin forever no matter how many times ur raped. U rape urself in hopes you won't be shocked again but you still do.

You start to spasm and I feel afraid bc I don't want u to die. U say this is what long term ketamine use does to your body and idk what to do bc I'm new with drugs and stuff.

U say pass me da vape I'm scared. Cloud my lungs. You lie face up and I feed u 5g clouds like I was your concubine and we were in an opium den. I am ur concubine and that is ok. Sorry feminists. I'm good with that. You say: *I could die rn.* It would be a beautiful way to die. Please don't. *But I could.* Ur an angel and a prophet so they will try to cancel u but that is not a good reason enough for you to die. You close your eyes, and you spasm, and I try to help you but I'm afraid of hurting you. You are so beautiful and I don't wanna forget. I think we kiss but I don't remember. I don't remember we have tongues or mouths to kiss.

Then I can't remember. Sleep seemed impossible but I think I fell asleep. Then we woke up and undid the sheets that seemed infinite last night. For the first time you say you are not hungry. For the first time I'm hungry in ur presence. So you eat blood sausages and I eat a lot of bread. We say goodbye. And I vomit on the bus.

/__/\

THE END

bestgore summer breeze

Sarah Ione Calcraft

bestgore summer breeze
jet fuel steel beams
boom clap
dry hump
alabama edgelord memes

creepy pasta sleepovers
ice cream on the covers
asbestos ceilings
missing pieces
adultery in adolescent lovers

the forest floor
stolen wine
ask everyone to come back to mine
if all my friends are here with me
then I can fall asleep tonight

bleach london
burning bath bitch
sandman cat scratch
baptised in bodymist
a vaporwave crystal witch

smoke a cigarette the wrong way round
bright blue dip dye
double crown

daily daisy chain reactions
golden haystacks black and brown

bouncy castles
chipped teeth
tall grass whispers unspoken grief
streetlights turn off at twelve
what was promised out of reach

no offence it was an awkward stage
a funny kind of uncomfortable age
the worst of it is over now
flick the killswitch
disengage

it was best gore summer breeze
broken bones
bleeding knees
the day that I became a woman?
the same day that I tried weed

buzzfeed and adult themes
so high and wasted
skinny jeans
brother's tshirts nazi zombies
bed fellows are strange indeed

youtube vlogging police sirens
belly laughs domestic violence
chatroom lockeroom conversations
boyband worship
facebook forums

online boyfriend
did you cheat
pedophile meet and greet
wait a second hold your tongue
virgin lips sticky sweet

best gore summer breeze
jet fuel
steel beams
turquoise coral hmv
teenage kicks teenage dreams

Bedroom Cowboy / Jesus Matchbook

Kaia Polanska Richardson

I'm horny, I'm stoned
Sitting pretty on the porch
Pretty come home   Please,
Pretty please.
I want to hear rocks under tires
I want dirt in my mouth
I want sweat in the air
And jeans soaked in dust
Dish soap hands pressed palm to palm
Held to chest in gentle prayer
Pray for cracked lips against my fingers
And your fingers in my hair
Tangled up   Make a mess
Trace the bruises + turn on the fan
Dance to its hum and pause

You sip your beer and light a dart
In my mouth, fall back on the bed
Like an Angel and I watch
Uncross my legs and
Wrap my arms around your head
                    Baby, I'm hot,
                    Pretty, I'm burning up.

Loogies

Quinn Adikes

There is a ferris wheel on the boardwalk where people go to spit. A few aim for the ocean, but most aim for the boardwalk. Some hit passersby and get into fights after being let off. The more polite spit when the walkway is clear.

Here, let's spit together: curl your tongue so it presses against the roof of your mouth. Gurgle until the mucus collects around your uvula. Once satisfied with the mucus collection, lower your tongue and push the mucus to the front of mouth. Swish the mucus around and mix it with the saliva and create what is known as a loogie. Don't let the loogie get runny. If the loogie gets runny it will break into small, unnoticeable pieces, which is the last thing anybody wants because to be noticed is to be alive. Once the mucus to saliva ratio feels correct, it is time to spit. Lean over the side of the gondola and purse your lips as if you are about to kiss your grandmother. Hopefully nobody is pushing a loogie while kissing their grandmother. And also nobody is kissing their grandmother. They are hawking loogies. In my opinion, hawking is the perfect verb for this scenario, but art should never explain itself, and so I will drop this image for you to interpret however you please: loogie dangling from the mouth like an icicle. Wind from the ocean blowing the loogie from side to side. Loogie breaking from the mouth and falling like bird shit. Loogie falling past other gondola riders: a single mother by herself, a tween couple very much in love, a garbageman and an ice cream man who hopes nobody will see them. Loogie narrowly avoiding the ferris wheel scaffolding. Loogie narrowly avoiding the flashing neon bulbs. Loogie narrowly avoiding a man sleeping on a bench. Loogie splattering by the ticket booth, and you are so far in the air but also you certain that you heard it. There are so many loogies glistening on these wooden planks and the owners of the boardwalk will never do anything to stop it. They know that loogies are the point.

What's So Bad About A Cult Anyways

Gillian Vernick

I understand why

people join cults

out here. something

about the cyan sky

makes me want to

believe. there's nothing

inherently wrong with a cult, right?

I remember that one summer

I almost got swept in.

I still miss fertile minds

luxe floor pillows

wafting palo santo

gathered buoyant heads
nodding silently
mumbled Tibetan chants

the contagion of belonging
infected me, an antidote
to rotting rituals.

What even is evil, anyways
I almost succumbed
so imagine you only

have hours to live
all life is emptiness
and everyone's waiting

for you there

in the swaying grasses

of your surrender.

Consent To Be Destroyed

Lauren Knabel

"Your honor, it's all right here—signed and dated,"

I, John Wayward, hereby consent to my death at the hands of, Isabella Demois, and assure that this was of my own volition. The perpetrator should not be held legally responsible in any capacity, and doing so would thus be a violation of my last dying wish.

The prosecutor rolled his eyes,

"Ms. Vontrese, you know that this is not a matter of whether or not your client wanted to kill Mr. Wayward, it's a matter of whether or not she liked it. You are trying to make it out like she had no choice. When she too signed off on this alleged consensual murder, making it, quite frankly, the most premeditated case of manslaughter I've ever seen."

You could feel the judgement radiating off of the minds of the jury.

I know that I'm supposed to appear brave, but every time I hear the cold legality of those words—meant only for paper, my soul convulses. I couldn't help but hide in my hair that morning. There is no latex or leather allowed in the courtroom after all.

***

Mr. Wayward was an unusual man and I mean that in the most uncomplimentary way possible. A Hollywood producer was who had the budget for a trophy wife or at the very least a sugar baby, yet he remained willfully alone. He had that type of pitiful charm that made you feel bad for him—but you hated it, because that sort of bartered empathy was exactly what he wanted. And Mr. Wayward always got what he wanted, even in death.

That day he came in reeking of cigarettes. Unusual but not entirely out of character. As several times he had me chain smoking cigarettes through a rubber tube into a mask strapped around his nose and mouth.

"Bad habits never die. Just find new forms," he'd often say.

A shaky hand held out that lethal document, the paper dampened with sweat. I could tell he was waiting for me to reply, making his big body small by hunching his shoulders. I know I shouldn't have been so curious, that I should've taken it as a cry for help, but you didn't know the John that I did. You didn't smell the eagerness of his sweat that day.

He smiled at my concern, scanning the red velvet walls lined with torture devices. His eyes fixed on the knives while saying,

"Why do you think I've been coming here for so long?"

He didn't wait for me to reply,

"I need to be punished, Bunny. The things I've done, no one should get away with... For years, I waited and waited for karma to finally catch up with me, but it never did. So I tested it, took matters into my own hands, but it never fixed it. That guilt, it gnawed away until my heart was no more than a pool of blood. But it's started to bite at my brain, in a way that even pain can't silence."

I thought of how he'd grin as the blade slid under his skin. His blood came so easily, with its red pity. How he would sigh in relief with each step of my stiletto, leaving scars on his spine like tallies for his unmentioned sins. Bleeding in between his legs. Thanking me for all that I've done. Still, my curiosity was not satiated.

"What exactly have you done John? All you talk about is how everyone walks all over you."

"Bad things, Bunny. Things I could never say to you until you sign that document."

"So you're really serious? you want me to kill you—right here, in the middle of LA?"

"You wouldn't have to deal with the body Bunny. My driver Jamie is outside waiting and he's ready to take care of it. I have a plot of land up in the redwoods. He's going to drive me there and bury me in my own land. I promise you, nobody will miss me enough to even care to find this document," he slid it closer to me with a delicate aggression.

"Please. Bunny, I need to die. And I need you to get it right this time."

"This time?!"

"Admit it. You don't not want to," he said, stepping closer to me, placing a grazing hand on my shoulder inches away from my neck.

"I gave her the chance. But she wasn't strong enough, not strong like you."

"Who's she?"

"She was always just in such a hurry. I had to get her to calm down. When she finally stopped crying I saw the violet handprints I'd left around her neck... But her eyes, Bunny—they looked more beautiful than I'd ever seen them."

I eyed my bag hanging on the door,

"Is this what you're looking for?" he said with more delight than I'd ever heard from him as he pulled out the hunting knife I carried with me at night. I tensed immediately, suddenly becoming Isabella again as I tried to take a step back. To which he tightened his grip on my clavicle and stopped me from going back any further.

Then handed me the knife,

"It's all yours now, Isabella. All of the power. You just have to finally be who you've been pretending to be. Or maybe, you're not as strong as I thought," he said while licking his chapped lips,

"Maybe you're just like them, pathetic and powerless when it comes down to i—"

I stabbed him in the gut—easier than I thought. The scene was gruesome as the blood seeped through his white button down shirt onto the floor. His expression of fatal surprise caused me to let out a deviant smile.

It was the perfect image of white-collared men and their need to be destroyed. Because they know they'll always hold the power. They say it's guilt, but that's bullshit. They enjoy making their pain my responsibility, projecting their demonized view of women so they can pretend it's real.

So I twisted the knife until I heard his arteries squelch, penetrating his chest over and over until I stopped having to feel his hot breath on my neck. When that initial smile wore off, the disgust at the warm and thick liquid pouring out at rapid rates caused me to freeze, horrified of who I had now become. It was the only thing left that I had never done and never wanted to do—kill someone. He stole that from me; my last sliver of innocence, my ability to sleep at night, my last hope at moral sanctity. I dropped the knife, as the gaping wounds in his abdomen surrounded him by an overflow of blood pooling from his heart, he said nothing, just moaned out of what should've been pain but didn't sound like it. Sitting there looking at me with a smirk of pure sadism and a visible erection, his eyes glazed over the same way they did after he'd finish, as he said his last words,

"Thank you Bunny, you did it. You saved me."

The boys next door

Ozziline Mercedes

The boys next door.
Their voices have become my alarm clock as they smoke cigarettes in their fluorescent uniform far too bright for 7am.
When I lean out my bedroom window, bed hair, half lit eyes, projecting "boyszszs" with the voice I usually reserve for the dungeon
as I glare at them with flirtatious order
because I know that's the only way to make them stop talking.

When I go to make my morning coffee, and later my lunch
I gaze at them from my kitchen window
cold morning spoon in my mouth as I eat a few mouthfuls of yoghurt, letting my mind wonder from fury that the council didn't tell us there would be year long construction right next to our house.
It isn't their fault, the boys next door.
They're just doing their job like the rest of us cursed Londoners.

I take this dirt
and get turned on by the terror that comes with tearing down a building so close to my head.
The vibrations of the earth's foundation that wake me from my dreams. Dreams of men

much softer than these boys
next door,
who slap me in the face with their demolition.
Those men and their diggers, their drills, the noisy machines of which I have no name for.
Thank god for my CBD vape
cutting my throat with its relaxing affect.
I look at their tools and think of all the things they could do to me. The ones with great big claws that cut through heavy metal.
All the things I could do with them.
If I knew how to.
Oh boy, to manoeuvre such a machine.

After lunchtime I hear them gossip about man things. I only pick up on certain words before their machines distract me with their aggressive hum again.

I wonder if they think I'm performing for them from the window as I walk in and out of my kitchen twenty times a day.
They don't know that I'm an artist / writer / erotic labourer who works from her bedroom with an undiagnosed attention deficit whose chronic stomach pain requires hourly herbal tea.
I saw one of them stretching the other day
leg up on debris.
His back arched the way stiff mans do.
The way my ex's had that time I put a butt plug inside him
one of glossy shiny metal before my flatmate

interrupted fisting my bedroom door.
I wondered if he knew I was watching, because he'd waved at me from the same spot the day before.
Later, I watched him clean his vehicle
cleansing the windows of its dusty filth.
There is an erotic dance to a man cleaning his ve-hhh-icle.
Like he's tending to his lover in a tenderly handsome way. His hand gripping the cloth as if it were her dress. His efforts as he pushes its softness against the glass, up and down, up and down, the way he might with her.

Delicious hard hats and heavy boots.
Another stood, hands down trousers.
He stared at the machines the way I do.
I wondered if he also finds their merciless purrrrr erotic
(his hand present for longer than a casual scratch).
Blokes like that will freely do such an act. Because they are mostly only observed by other blokes alike.
And their labour does not require them to act with a certain decorum.
And their uniform transcends individuality.
And their graft removes punishment.
The boys also have a very long hose with an ergonomically hand handle.
Elegant, actually.

I never knew demolition did that elegance.

Another type of dance that boys do
spraying water into the dust.
There is a romanticism to mixing these substances
a cleansing of filth for the sake of destruction.
Droplets falling with each broken edge.
They asked me what I do for a living when I knocked on their temporary door and asked to make a pact that they not wake me before 8am.

It's always good to flirt with manual labourers. Boys like them like bossy women like me. I've met many of them at work.

They looked at me like they knew my story, as if they saw the labour I do for boys like them.
Sex work is a form of manual labour,
really. In ways. We're both doing heavy lifting with our bodies.
Repetitive motions for
men with higher means. Men that tell us what to do with patriarchal authority, so they can send their kids to respectable schools and buy houses in the suburbs with gardens and kitchen islands.

"Many things," I said. Because if they knew I was up to no good in the bedroom above, who knows if I'd get any work done.
Perhaps they'd rev up their machines you see.
Or spray their hose into my window. In a horny language of the imaginary.

Imagining what was behind the wall they see
from down below, in a mating call of hard la-
bour
sensuality-y-y-y-
soaking my sheets and my t-shirt and my hair.
Because to them I am the girl next door.
And that would be so perfect, boys,
wouldn't it.

Dirty

Elisa Carini

I never thought I'd eat a person.

I tried being a vegetarian once. At school everyone was vegetarian (I went to art school), everyone smoked, and every Friday everyone went out to protest: pensions, deaths at work, famines, genocides, pollution, wars, pensions. I smoked every day and protested every Friday, and for two months and four days I stopped eating meat.

I decided I'd eat Noah while we were drinking at a bar called Dirty. I ordered a paloma with mezcal and a thick rim of salt. Noah ordered a raspberry liqueur.

I wondered if I'd taste it – the raspberry – when I bit into him, and Noah asked why I was making that disgusted face.

"What are you thinking about?"

"Nothing."

He went on telling me about the road trip with his friends in Croatia.

Maybe I'd taste it in his breath, on his tongue, but not in his blood or flesh.

"I hate raspberries."

Noah stopped talking. He said he was sorry.

"You were thinking about raspberries?"

I laughed. "Yeah."

The music was loud. Italian trap. The bar was dark, the lights bright red. Noah looked embarrassed. He probably thought my disgust meant we were going to fuck, that I'd hate his breath.

I turned his embarrassment into fear, and liked it better that way.

I laughed, again.

"Are you drunk?"

"A little."

When I bite off a piece of flesh, Noah screams. It's painful for me too because it's hard and I think I have a cavity somewhere. His blood is sweet. For a moment, I almost love him. Noah holds both hands on his neck and keeps screaming what the fuck are you doing, are you crazy? fuck, fuck, fuck and other curses full of "fucks".

His erection is gone. He looks at me in shock.

Milan at night is beautiful.

I never thought I'd eat a person.

When I tell the taxi driver, he thinks I'm joking.

Bodycount

Amaya Hopkins

Is it all violence from here on out? Virginities lost // To snuff film directors, weapons manufacturers

Father told me the rule of the brutes that // "If you kill someone, you better be ready // To carry that body with you the rest of your life."

Couldn't believe the words til I met those who were, // Ready for the extra soul weight, haunting of the scenes.

There's ghosts in the items now, and all is two-headed // Infected Chernobyl-like systems of affairs plague // My hope a radical satire. My trust is as serious as Genesis.

My perfume is slow explosions kaaaaaa boooooOOOM.

Glitter Bomb

Natalie Gilda

I'm an all pink glitter fairy bimbo
sinking my legs into and around
your waist,
telling you *I want to be alone with you*
upstairs
in the back
in a champagne room
no,
not in your apartment,
baby
please, baby
live in the fantasy
with me
do what you came
here to do
don't grind back against me
while I dance
baby,
that's my job
just let me do my job,
baby,
just let me
work.

When they beat the shit out of you, you loved it

Belinda Cai

In another world, you are wearing Brock Turner's skin. When the door opened and the first blow was dealt, it broke your nose and cracked your wireframe glasses.

You skid backwards onto the grass, fresh green stains on your jean pockets. You see him approaching and you don't even try to run.

Instead, you have an identity crisis.

Who are you? One day, you'll wake up as a credit analyst for a bank in the hometown you never left, balding and with no idea how to dress yourself. You'll remember your glory days, but not remember exactly how long ago they were.

Your sheltered, milquetoast, privileged suburban life bored you. This, no. This thrilled you.

He comes back and slams the side of your face into the dirt. Something warm is dripping down your cheeks, into the earth. He reaches for your pockets. You surrender.

You used to make jokes about "people like him," but yet, in this most unpredictable moment, you feel something that might be empathy or even love.

Maybe he needs what you have more than you do. Maybe you don't want what you have. Maybe you resent it. Maybe you despise it all. You laugh slowly, then you pick up the pace, like a crescendoing opera singer before the curtains fall.

It hurt so good. You'd never felt more alive.

pretty please

Ana Carrete

let's say i'm walking to my car after drinks // i powerwalk to it and look around // i take a video of myself and post it online for people to see // it only lasts a few seconds (no context)

living in the past is posting poorly-lit pictures

i post because it's dark and the parking lot is empty // only 4 or 5 cars are left on that level of the parking structure

i post the video because it's evidence // if anything bad happens to me // this video has been posted // and there are clues to use to find my body but yes // you're right i also want to show you my face // and you want to look at it

you are not the you in the poet's poem // stop fantasizing about being the you of everything // allow for characters to be other people who aren't you

in preschool a boy would tell me he was going to // marry me when we grew up and i hated him for it // I WAS ALREADY WIFEY MATERIAL // AND I WAS ONLY FOUR

you'd love to have my approval but it won't be easy // you won't impress me because i'm extra slow to warm up // if you like bad bitches that's good to know // i know you like them in theory and then you go sad mode // when you encounter a very bad one

there's clearly something wrong with me // *can you top that loser* // i can't accept compliments // i should have and express positive thoughts // i should be adorable but instead // i'm a conceited piece of shit

i don't care if irony as practiced and spoken // during the indie sleaze era // is cringe now // i love vintage // and friends told me to // never change

and when i'm high i'm passionate // about being earnest // and very very hot

felt ugly fought blemishes // failed to prevent future breakouts // zits turned into fine lines // acne came back ugliest hottest // colorizing pictures leaves your skin // glowing how many dimensions exist // what dimension is god in

steve aoki was the jesus of the indie sleaze era // but personally i prefer devon // 2 fast 2 furious sin city are you kidding me

A Spy in the House of Love

David San Miguel

Couldn't punch fast enough — REM atonia.

Zolpidem.

Nothingness.

The sun beats.

Escitalopram.

Warmth.

Joie de vivre.

A pit in the tummy.

No.

Just an empty stomach.

Pan Au Chocolat.

Ethiopian.

Marlboro Gold.

Methylphenidate.

Coherence.

Microdose self mythology.

Make it make sense.

Blue pill.

The healthy animal is up and doing.

Don't let it Hermann Nitsch you, little lamb.

Chills.

No.

A slight breeze.

Speech to text.

Moves tonight question mark.

The Hills.

Dead ass.

Love reaction.

Methylenedioxy-methylamphetamine.

Live fast.

Don't die.

Joy Williams for the soul.

Carson.

Bolaño.

Lispector.

Get the words out.

Inhabit them.

Benzo.

Bonne soirée.

Pay no worship to the garish moon.

Pick me up.

1942.

Neat.

Down the hatch.

C17H21NO4.

Pulverized.

Up the chute.

Pick me up.

Uber Black.

I have drunk the drug of forgetfulness.

Pick up the phone.

Pisces.

Password.

On the list.

Inside.

Inside me, there'll always be the person I am tonight.

Nothingness.

Fade to black.

Only God Can Save Me from Myself

Paige Vreede

We've had a few sleepovers before. It's mostly been spooning and a few cute kisses, an occasional dry hump like we were in 8th grade again, but last night was different. Last night we did the thing.

I arrive at midnight, the prime hour for a booty call, but with him, it feels ok, there's a confidence that I mean more than that. He tells me he's been lying in bed reading, and I tell him I packed my book as well. I curl up next to him, both with our novels in hand, and we spend the next 30 minutes reading in silence side by side as though we've been married 30 years and this is the part of the evening we don't exchange words.

He gets up to go pee, and when he comes back, he plants a kiss. It's the perfect amount of tongue and just enough saliva to be hot, but not sloppy. I could almost sense this was the night we'd go all the way. He makes his way to my neck, my breasts, my stomach. Finally, he reaches the holy grail. He goes around my panties as though my pink lace is some sort of chastity belt, knowing full well if they come off, we're doing the thing. I'm not sure if he's not sure, so I take them off myself. He moved close, almost reverent. In this moment, I feel both respect and pleasure, ease and ecstasy. Soon enough, I utter the words "Do you have a condom?" It's sweet. His arms wrapped around my shoulders, close, private, meaningful. He gets the job done, and I tell him he's "efficient." We laugh and intertwine our naked bodies.

An immense sense of guilt comes over me, as though I've just stolen a piece of his goodness. I lay my head on his bare chest and think of men before him: Men who didn't bother to ask if I wanted to use a condom, men who got off on aggressive thrusts from the back, men I lay next to counting the hours until we'd never speak again. The careless ones, the selfish ones, the ones who never asked, who made me feel like a placeholder in their stories. He wasn't like them.

I feel irresponsible with his emotions, but I don't want to assign myself that much power. I turn away, facing the wall where a framed image of the crown of thorns hangs above his bed.

I don't know which is more uncomfortable — being the woman lying here now, feeling like I've stolen a good man's innocence, knowing he's softer, and after all, a few years younger — or remembering the woman I've been, the one who wanted love so badly she mistook proximity for promise, lying beside men who would forget her by morning.

I'm in my mid-thirties. Isn't this the kind of person I should be pursuing? I think about how I don't even want to live in this country; it could never work. The self-sabotage is clear, abundant, ever-present. This feeling of fleeing something pure is familiar and unflinching I look up at the crown of thorns. Only God can save me from myself.

Summer Ketamine Ritual

Abby Romine

Over summer, I do ketamine 6 times in one week with an 80 year old anesthesiologist. He says we're fixing my hard drive. Pills are for software issues. Ketamine loves estrogen, he emphasizes. His sloth-covered office. A pretty girl like you, he says, should feel like a Disney Princess. I laugh, never showing my teeth.

The ritual goes as follows,

1. Eat a bowl of oatmeal. Drink a small yellow Gatorade. Arrive.

2. Public restrooms circle Hell. Pee in Hell.

    a. Avoid pissing your pants in Not Hell.

3. Enter a cold room. Accept a white blanket. Use the same vein. Turn off the lights.

4. Take a flash photo. Send it to your mother.

5. Feel close to God for an hour. Understand. It's all so simple. Simple, but still.

    a. Bailey tells me sex on ketamine is supposed to be really intense. He knows exes that fell back in love after it. I tell him, that makes sense. On ketamine I'm in love with everyone.

6. Drink water from a paper cup. Walk back to the restroom. Pee. Still coming down.
Take a flash photo in the mirror. Attach yourself to reality. Send it to your mother.

7. Depart.

    a. Go shopping. See a bunny. Name it Context.

    b. Get lost. Go home.

8. In bed. Pour over hundreds of screenshots.

    a. Laugh. Then cry. And sleep.

    b. Wake up wanting.

According to an arbitrary rating system after each session, I am 11% better. I clap a gnat to death. A big boom for a minuscule thing. The acupuncturist loses a needle in me. The Uber has fake grass for a floor. He wishes me good luck in all my beginnings. But it's my ends that need the wishing. It's that quarter of my soul, stolen by a cokehead highschooler in 2010. Three quarters of a wish.

1000 recetas de amor

Lucci Garcia

Must start writing stories like poems,
as always, saying without saying,
telling
without telling.
Speak of desire, of rejection, of disappointment,
of the breakfasts and the endless clouds,
of the illusion and the deception of August,
of passion, shame, nerves, blood, pain, air and wind,
the waves,
the concert, the night—
but above all, speak of dreams.
Of the good and the bad you told me.

You think you know me better than I do,
but honey, I know myself better than you know you.
The witchcraft and the spell you'll feel—
or not.
And
merely the uncertainty.
Was the time spent on you something lost,
a lesson,
or someone dead about to cross over?
A moment looking at the northwestern sea.
I won't cry,
I won't cry for what I've learned
but for what I haven't lived.

We will have time to learn how to make love.

And you walked away because of my
madness,
but you don't know what it means to be mad.

Bathtime

Mary Morgan

If they make monsters of men we must make terrors of ourselves.

I have an insatiable lust for blood.

I sit in my house, legs splayed wide on the wooden floor, the sun blasting through the windows as a train screeches along tracks within eyeshot and earshot, twirling a knife in my hands, closing my eyes to feel the distinct weight of the blade versus the handle, flipping it over, and over, until it is an extension of my hand, a new growth that I am the first to develop, a simple evolutionary need for these monsters, for every monster needs a slayer.

I practice throwing it at the white walls. I grew up throwing knives. I apologize in my head to the walls, for they have done nothing to deserve this, but, as I explain to them, I cannot practice outside, for I live in a city, and I cannot risk (1) hitting something living or (2) being carted off to some other white-walled room much less pleasant than this sun-dripped one.

Have you ever cleaned blood out of a bathtub?

The first time I cleaned blood out of a bath was easy enough. I stepped into the porcelain. The red liquid oozed down my breast bone, pooling in my belly button, dripping down my thighs until it made little ski slopes down my shins and calves. Red circled the drain, changing color as it diluted itself with the hot water, fading from darkness to light, much as I had felt that night's actions had done, faded some darkness into light.

There is still a spot of blood on the ceiling above the shower. It would be so easy to clean but I like it there. I'm not sure whether as a reminder or a warning.

The next time, I rented a hotel room specifically for my monster slaying. I did not want to taint, literally and figuratively, my own bath with delicious redness.

There was so much more blood to clean that time, my body morphing from its natural warm-undertone honey beige to scarlet, a crimson person emerging from the lagoon. Leaving red footprints as I fetched a bottle of cremant from the mini fridge in the bedroom.

There is no more euphoric bath than bathing in the blood of your enemies.

However, the cleanup, not so ideal. I'm a horrendous cleaner at best, anyone can tell you, it's really not my strong suit. But it's rather important for this type of work. I was a novice at the time, and did not account for the sheer amount of grout that was in this particular bathroom.

If you are ever to follow in my bloody footsteps, let me warn you, choose your bathrooms wisely.

Do not choose one with teeny tiny tiles all over the walls with white grout in between them.

Anyway so there I was, hot with blood and hot from the bath and hot from the bottle of bubbles I slammed, on my hands and knees scrubbing fucking blood out of about oh I don't know thousands of tiles. I wore down all of my nails. After about three hours I no longer saw red, and went to bed. The next morning, I turned the lights on in the bathroom, and it was like one of those scenes from a horror film, fucking blood still everywhere, my eyes had apparently stared at the color for so long I had neutralized it and didn't see it any more the night before. So another three hours of cleaning and I thought, well, that's as good as it's going to get, and stole all the now red towels, and fled that hotel. Safe to say I am very much not welcome back there.

I tell all of this to you, dear reader, for I am curious if you are a monster or a slayer. If you're like me, please, come to me, and I'll teach you how you too can grow a knife from your veins, forged of your own heartbeat and their blood. I await your reply.

But If you're a monster. you'd better start running. Monsters think they're a darkness but they're merely a shadow. I am the night. I will swallow you whole and leave no trace. Nothing but a drop of blood on my lips. And maybe on my ceiling.

Chucklefucker

Sascha Cohen

I.

Confirmed CIA asset Gloria Steinem once wrote,
we are becoming the men we wanted to marry
So I must be putting on my clown makeup,
smeared joker grin spreading
from hoop earring to hoop earring.

II.

Groupies were the original frackers
extracting liquid energy and trading it
back and forth between each other,
five straws digging into one milkshake.
Am I right?

III.

I survey the green room's innards
for the roundest, sweatiest man
with hopes to be his prize.
I throw my head back and laugh.
I lick the rubber soles of his Vans.
I hope I'm invited to Canter's after this!

IV.

Does anyone else love to feel tarnished?
You, in the back?

V.

Unzip the pants of any headliner

and find a pink balloon animal. Find
a plastic chicken. Find emotionally
immature parents. Look up and find
your own face, bruised with rainbow grease-
paint.

VI.

I used to be a piece of ass, Eve Babitz wrote
on a sign she hung on the door
of her Formosa Street apartment.
But now I'm an artist.

Well I've never read *Slow Days, Fast Company*
but I've seen Eve nude
in that photo, playing chess. I've seen her
pendulous white breasts, and I think
they're beautiful

i love u and u r safe

Annabelle S. Baird

There is a video on YouTube that Honey watches every night called Mommy Cleans Your Ears RP.

The video advertises itself as a comforting sleep aid.

The soft sounds and gentle whispers are supposed to lull you into rest without reminding you that you are watching a woman pretend she is your mommy through the vortex of the internet.

People in the comment section say this video has saved their lives on their darkest days.

Honey cannot help imagining herself as a little boy watching the video. She does not think the concept works if she is not a little boy.

Honey is a 22 year old woman. As she watches the video, she sits in her bedroom with fairy lights that she never turns off.

When mommy asks what pajamas Honey wants, she always picks the green and blue dinosaur ones. She gets frustrated when mommy chooses the pink bunny nightgown for her instead.

Honey sometimes masturbates to the video even though she knows she is not supposed to.

Sometimes she thinks she is supposed to but mommy would never admit it.

Honey's real mommy works the night shift at a museum. Honey's daddy teaches eighth grade Algebra and sometimes freshman geometry.

Honey types in the comment section.

> 2 WHOEVER'S READING THIS
> KNOW I LOVE U AND U R SAFE <3

She deletes the comment.

> KYS

She deletes the comment.

> HAII \(> ᴗ <)/♡

She looks at the comment and leaves it there. Three people heart her comment.

Mommy is cleaning her ears now with Q-tips and cotton balls. Honey watches from the minimized picture-in-picture box as she scrolls through recommended videos.

LENS LICKING 4 YOUR PLEASURE

3-DIO MIC EAR KISSES

SHH HOLDING YOU AND
TOUCHING YOUR FACE AS YOU
FALL ASLEEP

Suddenly a pop-up appears on Honey's aging 2020 era Macbook.

YOU'VE BEEN PHISHED! CLICK HERE TO REVERSE THE DAMAGE! CLICK ! CLICK! CLICK! CLICK! CLICK!

Honey clicks because what else is she supposed to do.

There is bukkake on her screen.

Honey closes her laptop and after a few minutes of tossing and turning, she drifts off to sleep. Honey dreams about being forced to wear a pink bunny nightgown.

Honey's laptop slides off her bed as she shifts in her sheets, resisting mommy pulling the nightgown over her head. The laptop hits her surge protector knocking the fairy lights' plug out of an outlet.

Everything goes dark.

Honey's room goes up in flames.

JELL-O/Everyone Is Holding Hands in the Blockchain

Michaella Sangiolo

turn me on
i mean for work
flick red go button
plastic tongue
i was eating
jell-o and oatmeal
when they let me go

corporate plank walk in
thrifted loafers
designed to make my ankles baby
break
for the bosses, liability
in white socks

i thought being grown up
meant getting laid
all the time
instead it means
proximity to evil

plastic cuts
off the rim of
a twenty dollar salad
the seams of a gaze
up the back of a pair

of legs
blood never red (real)
until it hits the air

i know blood is made of cells
floating in darkness
and the cells have
little personalities
little jobs
a corporation
oxidizing
pumping towards
oblivion

all offices could be porn sets
i listen to my music
behind a shiny desk
it's easy to imagine i'm the same
as a lamp
or a door stop
cunt out
on top
of the shiny desk

one of those
nice girls
suspended in
lime green jell-o
one of those
girls
that get paid
to lie down
and be eaten off of

flesh on flesh on flesh
like in the movies

my job is
availability telegraphed
by the symmetry of
parting appendages
ready to receive
information

mostly though
my job is receipts
which are like
blood oaths across
a line of
credit

the data here
is pure sugar
pure oracle
the rounds and rounds and rounds
of drinks
2AM doordash orders
i love
the nakedness of these men
their paper slip (ups)

there are lots of words
for god
capital
daddy
saturn
is

a hole
in the universe
a paper cut
slashed across
my finger prints

a kiss between objects
an exchange of dna
and then everything
begins again as
alpha deployed across
several diverse vehicles

Martinis are an indicator of growth

Erika Tanahashi

Martini glasses make me feel clumsy in an adolescent way // Like a child sipping sprite from a wine glass

I am cosplaying an adult // In second hand knee high leather boots and $50 lipgloss

I wonder how I've gotten this far in life without being able to properly drink a martini

The first few sips splash against my upper lip aggressively // The rim is just as wide as a devious smile // Drenching my chin with dribble // So I lap it like a dog

My lips glazed and coated...sugary....sticky // I can't seem to hold the shallow glass steady // My fingers trembling // Feel adhesive

I suck on them // I make three seconds of eye contact with four people // While I suck on them

This gives me great pleasure // Because I know I still look hot

I feel exposed to these strangers though //

They are voyeurs to my shame // My body's refusal to mature // My cheeks prickle with heat from the alcohol // And embarrassment...

I think about how a dick would taste...and feel on my sanitary tongue

Honestly this whole entire time at the bar // The sloppiness of it all // I've been thinking about sucking dick

Swingers, Sinners

Matthew Tyler Vorce

In Los Angeles you can see some strange things.

A gang member is eating a chef's salad alone talking about "The Bears" to anyone who will hear him.

An Asian man sits four chairs down wearing the gangs sigil, unbeknownst to him.

He works in tech and drives a Tesla. "A Tessie."

He tells the waitress, "You dont even have to press the brake for it to stop. It just stops. Elon baby!"

When he honks his horn "Drop It Like It's Hot" plays. He has more money than my entire family combined.

The waitress has blisters. She has three jobs not counting Onlyfans. It was booming during Covid, but now it's just creeps.

It was always just creeps.

I ask her if I can have more coffee but she

doesn't hear me. The ghosts of Beverly Drive have her now.

I'm supposed to be meeting a girl from the canyon whose future lives somewhere in the valley of those hills. In the secret tunnels maybe she will find herself. David Lynch could have a field day in her head.

Across the room a man says, "I expect theater to come back in a BIG way."

"Oh." says his friend.

A table of four gays ordered four Oreo shakes as soon as they sat. Doubled down on the theater comment and now they are comparing favorite plays.

I swear I heard someone say Hadestown seriously and the table fell quiet.

I've never seen it, but with context clues that

might be a faux pas.

More gays just got here.

The Hadestown comment really seemed to dampen the mood.

I try and cheer them up and they just glare at me.

My friend is now an hour late, and if she was on time I couldnt have written this.

Maybe it's fate.

Maybe I'm always running a little bit late.

The last time I was at this restaurant I was with a girl that I loved.

We shared a BLT with mayo on the side. She prefers mustard.

I think about her a lot. Almost always.

I think her TikTok reposts are hidden messages just for me. But she hates me.

She told me.

Three times.

Sometimes when I look at my hand long enough I can start to see through it.

I start to wonder if other people can see through me also.

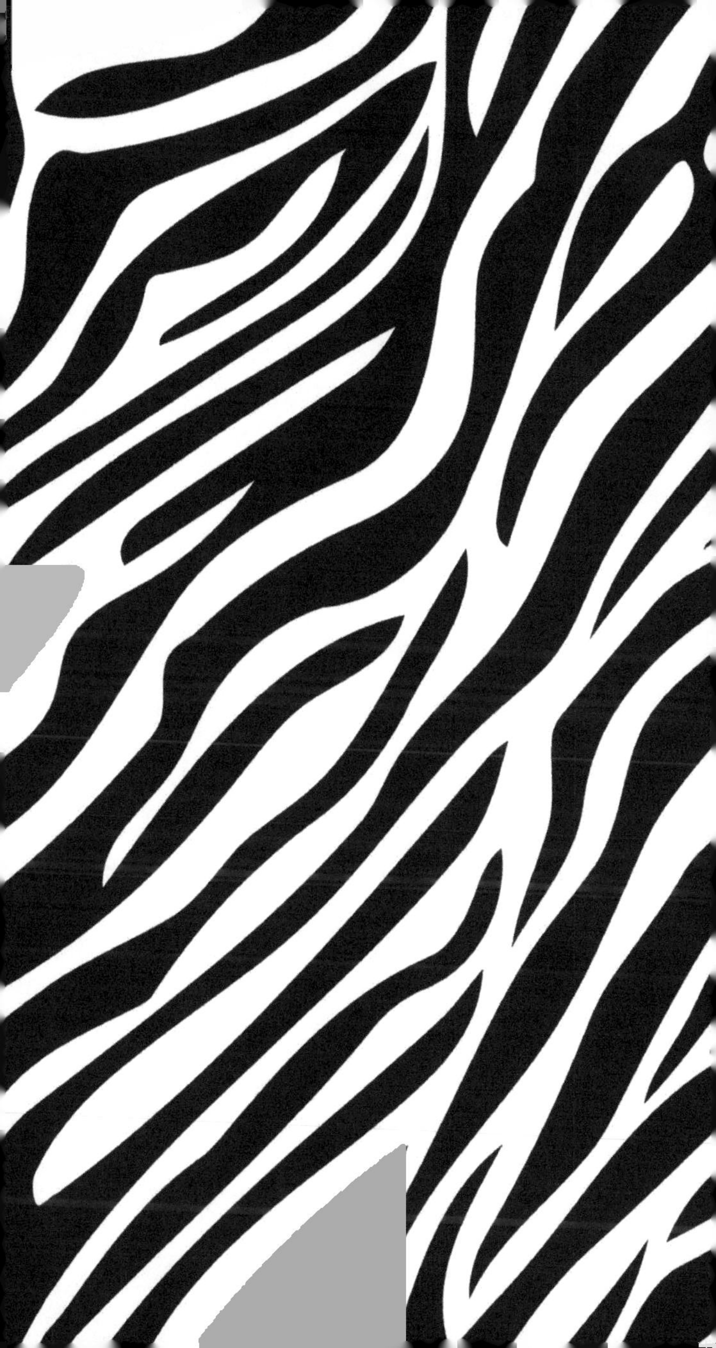

2 April 2025 at 12:25pm

Sofia Insua

i wanna make u a platter of freshly cut
fruit
drive you to the coast
- foreign license plate -
right down to the pacific ocean to show u
the dark
i'll pour lime juice onto ur everything
the coconut water i've cut right out of the
palm tree
the paper-cut on your finger
the blister on ur heel
the deep cut of our love when i leave this
june
(the pain would b fresh and tropical)
but don't worry
i'll throw u right into the salty water of El
Paredón – where all the gringos go –
and it'll help the scarring
cause the salt in the water is good for you
especially the wounds
and then you can say you've been down to
Guatemala

Mirror Girls

Emily Leibert

The mirror girls always go looking for themselves. They are looking at their reflections in an Alo storefront, in the trio of lenses on the back of an iPhone, in the cyborgs that star in the videos they post on TikTok. The big lie is that it is vanity which keeps their heads down, busy with all this obsession, this excessive self-recognition. That's fiction, too — that girls of the technology age used all that information potential to stare dumbly at themselves with puppy dog ears and strawberry freckles and doughnut-glazed skin. That's not how it is. The mirror girls have been poked through with holes. They are trying to stave off the emptiness. They are looking to confirm that they are still real. When they're not drenched in all that blue, I don't know. I just don't.

The Real Movement

Gulen Celik

The veil shook me to my core. Suddenly my inner cogs were no longer in rust, rather an imprint of smile appeared on each of my cells which opened up the desire for a sexy scientist to look through the microscope and declare, with reverence, this is The Real Movement. The practice of my words was like fencing in a moldy stone castle — I had to be careful both with brute and grace. My posture changed, my rhythm started to know itself and how it moved along with the rest of the world. I wanted to reach a universal dictionary to have access to every portal of promise and appearance, to tap into the collective records of boundless wisdom and blow it effortlessly like a little girl does to a dandelion with innocent saliva mixed, DNA breeding possibilities of love, more love, love, love... World peace felt, for a ridiculous moment, like it might actually be located somewhere near the collarbones, tapping there and under your eyes to stimulate the blood vessels, to establish direct contact with your very own unfathomable living mechanism, to write what will be half-read in between someone's transitory yet somehow never ending half-lived period of life, maybe during a work break of oral fixation, a sinister distraction and a celebration of the schizophreniac feedback loop. Her's and His mugs and masks; fake loyalty creating a kingdom of casualties, inner compass losing the edge of certainty and assertiveness for the next tyranny of validation. The harsh truth is that when the body thinks you are divided within, you become an insufferable person with all sorts of loathsome symptoms and over-extensions of petty breaches. Breathing is the only validation so I sing myself forward. Some say you don't need faith for this. Just remember that every system, biological or digital, survives by exchange. Give heat, receive light. Notice when you're closed, reopen. The smallest acts, making coffee, touching another wrist, looking up from the screen to the sky are maintenance rituals for the infinite. But faith gives you permission to answer those moments without irony. To say thank you into the air, not knowing to whom but sensing a face there. To act as if love were a law of thermodynamics, wisdom beyond your exhaustion.

Gwenyth Paltrow Writes a Story

Sophie Gillet

Gwenyth Paltrow sits at her desk after a full three days of being sick. She is about to write a revolutionary article for her blog. During these treacherous hours, Gwenyth has not been able to 'eat clean.' She even took a Tylenol. No need for that hefty spoonful of Manuka Honey tonight!

At first she is ashamed, but Gwenyth works through her self-deprecation to uncover a new, more exciting feeling: pride. She is just as frail and weak-willed as all of the other, lesser humans who rely on big pharma! This makes Gwenyth relatable! She realizes that not even the jade ball in her specialplace can save her from her sad, fragile human state. And as we all know, misery adds great worth to the soul of a person, which is why it must be flaunted and written about whenever possible.

And Gwenyth certainly does write. She begins a passage about her life-changing experience after taking the Tylenol–the one in which she realizes she is a person like the rest of us. IT'S OKAY! Her head is throbbing. IT'S OKAY NOT TO EAT CLEAN SOMETIMES. ALLOW YOURSELF TO EAT BREAD, SOMETIMES.

Her fingers are shaking and her temples are pulsing. yes. She whispers to herself, her coconut oil spittle falling onto her white linen shirt. yes, this is transformative. yes, this will change the world. Gwenyth's face slowly begins to change. She is turning into John Keats. Her epiphany has allowed her to achieve a deeper understanding of life. John Keats types, deeply and poetically.

IT'SOKAYTOHAVEATYLENOLATYLENOLTHATSBLUEBLUEBLUELIKEANORCHIDINTHESUNLIKETHEWINDWHENIFEELITSTENDERMELANCHOLYINTHEMOSTINTIMATEHOURSOFTHENIGHTSOBLUE–

Suddenly, John Keats stops typing because Gwenyth's Rich Plastic Shaman has arrived. The Rich Plastic Shaman enters the room and sees John Keats.

GWENYTH! WHAT IS GOING ON GWYNETH! YOU DON'T LOOK LIKE YOU'RE LIVING A HIGH VIBE LIFE GWENYTH! YOU DON'T LOOK LIKE YOURSELF AT ALL! LET'S GET THOSE SILLY THOUGHTS OUT OF YOUR HEAD! OH YES, YOU ARE SO TORTURED GWENYTH! YOU ARE MORE TORTURED THAN ANY OTHER HUMAN, AND THAT'S WHY YOU'RE SPECIAL! YOU DESERVE TO RELAX! YOU DESERVE TO CLEAR YOUR HEAD OF ALL OF THESE

NASTY LITTLE HUMAN THOUGHTS! YOU OWE IT TO YOUR SOUL! TO YOUR SPIRIT GUIDES! TO YOUR CELESTIAL–

John Keats screams and withers into dust. Gwenyth is reborn from the ashes.

YOU'RE SO RIGHT. OH MY DEAR PLASTIC SHAMAN, YOU'RE SO RIGHT. I WAS FALLING INTO A TRAP. I WAS NOT LIVING A HIGH VIBE LIFE. I WAS LETTING MY HUMAN SELF INTERFERE WITH MY WELLNESS. I WAS NOT FLOATING ABOVE ALL PEOPLE, LIKE A BEAUTIFUL ANGEL. PLEASE TAKE THIS MONEY. TAKE ALL OF THIS MONEY SO THAT YOU CAN KEEP TEACHING ME HOW TO BE BETTER. LOOKING AT THE SCUM DOWN BELOW. I'LL NEVER TAKE A TYLENOL AGAIN. I'LL NEVER EAT BREAD AGAIN. I'LL SMOKE MY WEEKLY CIGARETTE, BUT THAT'S IT. OH, RICH PLASTIC SHAMAN, YOU ARE SO WISE. THANK YOU FOR NOT LETTING ME FALL INTO THE TRAP OF MY OWN DISGUSTING HUMANITY. THANK YOU FOR WIPING ME CLEAN OF EVERYTHING THAT COULD POSSIBLY AFFECT ME.

I Don't Have to Write a Poem

Tess Nealon Raskin

To know you really did some damage this time.
I have tucked myself under the bed.
Through the floorboards I can see my house
In the distance, the plastic piping, bright blinds
I never quite found familiar. I woke her from
the dark doorway and she must have thought
I was four again. The mark from where you
Soaked through my shirt. Your voice in my ear
and my back trembled open. Head plummeted
down the shoot towards my feet. The second
Time someone gave me a pill, your voice curl
ing like smoke. Now everything is quiet.
I had something
  then I lost it.
Say no to the fast car of misery. *Love you*
somewhere in the overheads. Might never be
quite used to this.

www.ingramcontent.com/pod-product-compliance
Lightning Source LLC
LaVergne TN
LVHW021156160826
845679LV00024B/2141

* 9 7 9 8 9 9 2 0 6 6 3 4 0 *